This

DINOSAUR ROAR!

™

book belongs to

....

For my little monsters

Ten Terrible Dinosaurs first published in 1997
This edition first published in 2017 by Macmillan Children's Books
an imprint of Pan Macmillan
20 New Wharf Road, London N1 9RR
Associated companies throughout the world
www.panmacmillan.com

ISBN 978-1-5098-3552-2

1 3 5 7 9 10 8 6 4 2

A CIP catalogue record for this book is available from the British Library.

Printed in China

TEN
TERRIBLE
DINOSAURS

PAUL STICKLAND

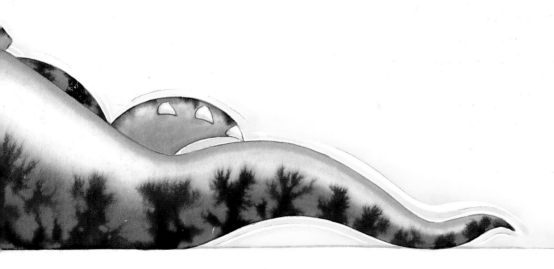

MACMILLAN CHILDREN'S BOOKS

 **10** Ten terrible dinosaurs

standing in a line,

soon began to mess about,

until there were . . .

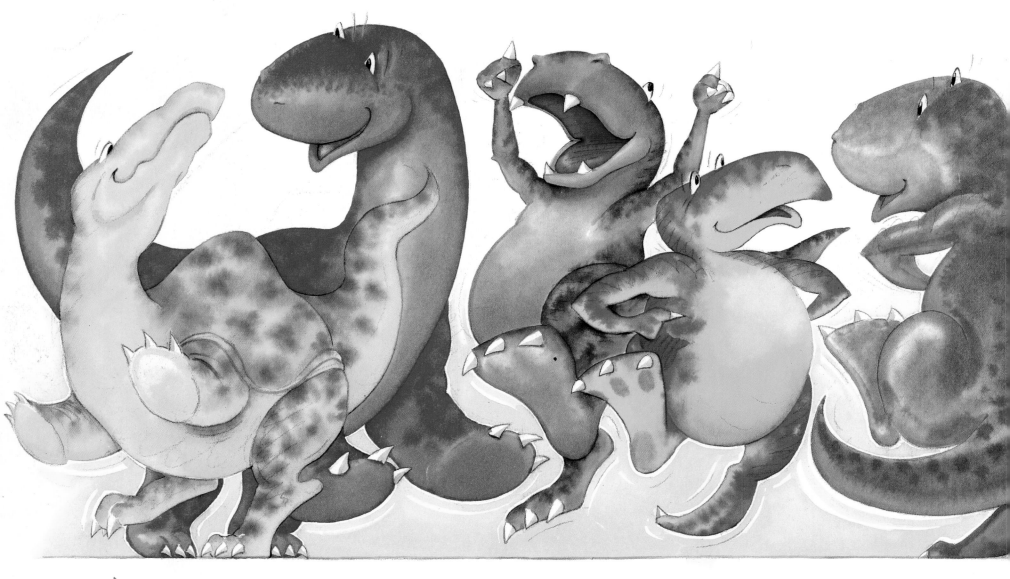

 **9** Nine enormous dinosaurs,

their dancing was just great,

but one was much too spiky,

so soon there were . . .

8 Eight elated dinosaurs

thought they were in heaven,

but one nearly popped,

so then there were . . .

 **7** Seven silly dinosaurs

playing silly tricks

one went wrong,

so then there were . . .

6 Six stamping dinosaurs

did a crazy jive,

one got tangled up,

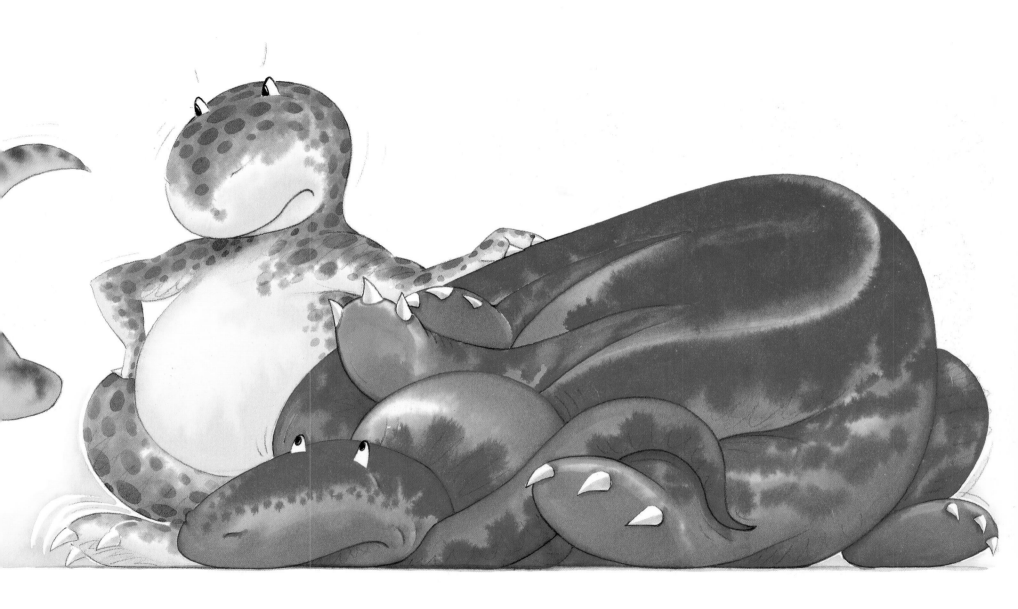

so then there were . . . .

 **5** Five feisty dinosaurs,

fierce in tooth and claw,

one's mum said, "STOP THAT!"

so then there were . . .

4 Four fearless dinosaurs

hiding in a tree,

one got stuck,

so then there were . . .

 **3** Three eager dinosaurs

tried and almost flew,

one really did,

so then there were . . .

 **2** Two tetchy dinosaurs,

far too tired to run,

one got taken home,

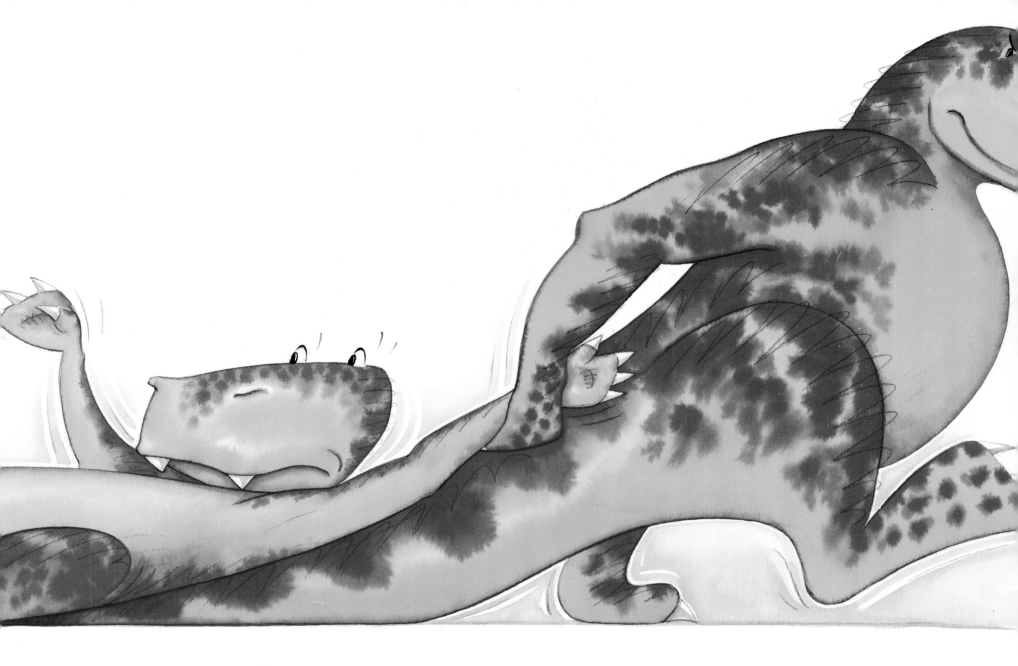

so then there was . . .

 **1** One weary dinosaur

soon began to snore,

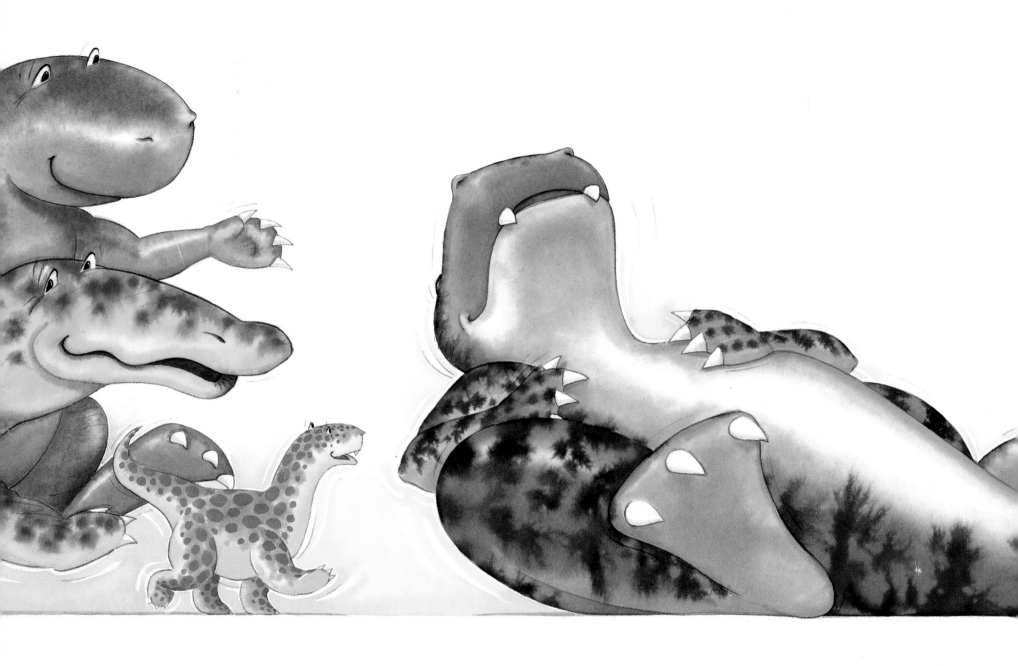

his friends crept up on him

and suddenly yelled . . .

RO

Can you count the dinosaurs?

1

2

3

4

5

Look out for more

DINOSAUR ROAR!

titles from Macmillan

Reviews of Dinosaur Roar!

". . . the picture-book giant for small children . . . one of my favourite books ever to read out loud."

The Times

"The simplicity and comforting rhythms make this instantly appealing."

Independent on Sunday

Visit **www.dinosaurroar.com** for more dinosaur fun!